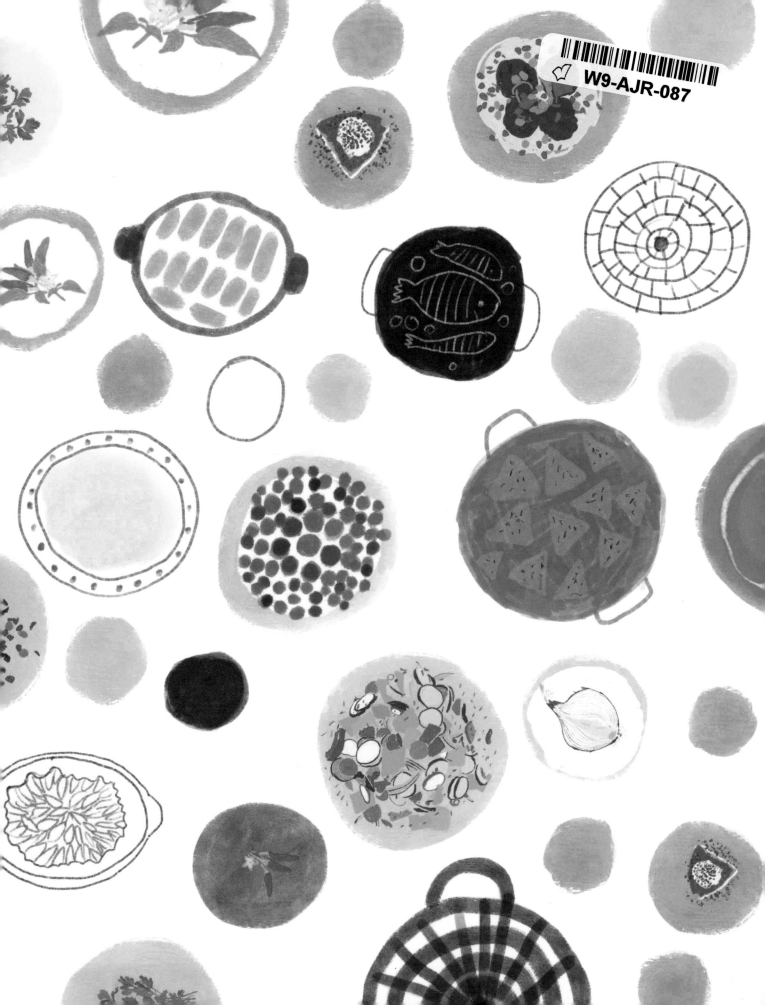

Arab Fairy Tale Feasts

A Literary Cookbook

First published in 2021 by CROCODILE BOOKS
An imprint of Interlink Publishing Group, Inc.
46 Crosby Street, Northampton, Massachusetts 01060
www.interlinkbooks.com

Published simultaneously in Canada by Tradewind Books

Library of Congress Cataloging-in-Publication Data available
ISBN 978-1-62371-908-1

Art direction by Carol Frank
Book design by Elisa Gutiérrez

The text of this book is set in Archer and Sofia Pro.
Titles are in Paquita Pro

10 9 8 7 6 5 4 3 2 1

Printed and bound in Korea

Arab Fairy Tale Feasts

A Literary Cookbook

Tales by **Karim Alrawi**

Recipes by **Sobhi al-Zobaidi & Tamam Qanembou-Zobaidi**
and **Karim Alrawi**

Illustrations by **Nahid Kazemi**

Crocodile Books, USA

An imprint of Interlink Publishing Group, Inc.
New York • Northampton

To Asma, who enchanted my childhood with her stories and
left me with enduring memories of times together in the kitchen; to
Suzanne, who shared those times with me; and to Maysa, who will
one day be old enough to write her own recipes and stories. —KA

To our daughters, Kenza and Maleekah: You bring joy
to every meal we eat together, and your jokes
about our cooking will never be forgotten. —S&T

CONTENTS

The Meal and the Conversation

"Nothing heals the body like a good meal, and nothing soothes the soul like a good story."

THIS ARAB APHORISM, OR SAYING, seems like a good way of welcoming you to *Arab Fairy Tale Feasts*, the latest in our series of international storied cookbooks. And, as always, after the welcome comes the introductions. So, who are Arabs and why a cookbook?

The word Arab applies to people who mainly live in North Africa and the Middle East. This includes the southern and eastern rim of the Mediterranean, the land around the Red Sea and the Arabian Peninsula. Arab people live in diverse communities with long histories and many different beliefs and customs. What unites us is a culture formed around a common language called Arabic. It is a book culture, as Arab lands have been home to some of the world's most famous libraries, from ancient to modern times. These include the libraries at Fez in Morocco, Kairouan in Tunisia, Alexandria and Cairo in Egypt, Antioch in Syria, Baghdad in Iraq and the Zaydi and Abadi libraries of Yemen and Oman.

The earliest collection of recipes we know of was written on clay tablets in the ancient Akkadian language. Akkadian is older than the Arabic and Hebrew languages. These first recipe tablets were created around 1700 BCE by an ancient people called the Babylonians who lived in what is now the country of Iraq. The writing of cookbooks in Arabic is also an old tradition, going back at least a thousand years. Some of the earliest cookbooks we know about were written in the tenth century. Famous Arabic recipe books were written in what are now the countries of Egypt, Morocco, Spain, Syria and Iraq. One of the most famous, also written in the tenth century, was simply called *The Cookbook*. It was written by an author named Ibn Sayyar al-Warraq. Copies of al-Warraq's book have survived and so we have a good idea of his recipes, savory and sweet, and the rules of the kitchen in his time.

The golden age of Arab cookbooks was between the tenth and thirteenth centuries. One book, called *Scents and Flavors*, also included recipes for hand soap and body deodorants made with violets and sandalwood. A fourteenth-century Egyptian cookbook, *The Treasure Trove of Benefits and Variety at the Table*, included recipes for washing powders made with camphor and citronella, two strong-scented essential oils.

These cookbooks served a double purpose. They were both a collection of recipes and a source of nutritional advice. Other cookbooks were written by physicians and included advice on the order that courses in a meal should be served to improve health and digestion. The order recommended in these books became the standard we know today: starting a meal with soup or salad, then a main course followed by a dessert of fruit or sweet pastries. Washing one's hands before and after meals was considered both polite and hygienic. While it was common in Europe for the poor to eat mainly vegetables and the rich to eat meat, the Arabic cookbooks recommended a varied diet. Good cookbooks were so highly regarded that one was even written by a sultan (an Arab king), Ibrahim ibn al-Mahdi, in the ninth century.

Some foods we think of as European have their roots in early Arab cuisine. *Paella* is a Spanish dish of saffron rice with vegetables and meats. Paella is well-known as being from the city of Valencia in Spain, which was an Arab princedom for almost 500 years. In Arabic the same dish is called *baeyah*, which means leftovers. Saffron, a fragrant spice first grown in Iraq, means "golden leaves." The word saffron comes from the Arabic *zafaran*.

Pasta, one of the most famous foods of Italy, is made from durum wheat. In North Africa, durum wheat grows in an arid, or dry, climate. It is used to make couscous, a staple of many North African meals. Durum wheat was brought to Europe by Arab traders through Sicily and Spain. It was ground and made into flat sheets of pasta, similar to lasagna. The word "lasagna" itself comes from the Arabic word *lesan*, meaning "tongue." In fact, the earliest accounts of pasta-making are in an Egyptian cookbook from the tenth century.

The Arabs also brought recipes to Europe that they learned from other cultures. For example, *al-sikbaj* is a fish or meat dish they learned from the Persians. It is called *escabeche* in Spain and *ceviche* in Latin America. Early on, Arab traders mastered the seasonal pattern of winds, commonly called trade winds, linking the Arabian Peninsula with India, Indonesia and the Far East, as well as Africa. They brought spices to Europe from those distant lands. Many spices still have names that are similar to their names in Arabic: cumin from *kammun*, caraway from *karawya*, tarragon from *tarkhoon*, and ginger from *janzabil*.

To end on a personal note, I would like to explain the choice of recipes for this book. I was brought up in a household of women. My mother was a great dessert cook, but not so good with savories. Her creations in the kitchen were often experiments not to be repeated. One memorable example is her zucchini and tuna omelet. My aunt Asma often spent weekends with us. She was a wonderful cook, and enjoyed having my sister and me help her in the kitchen. I have included some of her recipes along with those provided by Tamam and Sobhi.

In writing this book, we have tried to follow the old tradition of great Arab cookbooks by offering a combination of recipes, illustrations and stories to give the flavor of Arab culture. There is a saying in Arabic: "To join a conversation while sharing a meal makes for the best of times." So, in the spirit of this aphorism, please think of the stories here as the start of a conversation, and the recipes as an offering in place of a meal. We hope you enjoy sharing your time with us, as we enjoyed preparing this book for you.

Juicy Apricots

Once there was, though maybe not, a young girl named Malak who lived in a city called Marrakesh, in Morocco, at the foothills of the Atlas Mountains. Often, when she went for walks, she would pass a garden with a great apricot tree whose lovely golden apricots caught the sun. Around the garden was a tall fence. At one end of the garden, the fence was low enough for her to climb. And so, one day, when the apricots were amazingly large and juicy and just wouldn't stop calling her, she climbed the fence.

Once in the garden, she realized the apricots were too high for her to reach. She pulled herself up on a branch. She picked an apricot and ate it. It was ever so sweet and tasty, and the juice ran down her chin. She climbed farther up the tree to get to the ripest fruit. She tasted one and it was so yummy. She climbed up another branch and then another. Once at the top of the tree, she picked more apricots and stuffed them into the pockets of her skirt. She thought, when she got home, her mother could make apricot pudding for her. After Malak had collected enough of the fruit, she decided it was time to leave. But when she looked, she saw how far she was from the ground and couldn't see a way to climb down. *Oh dear, I'm doomed,* she thought.

When eventually the gardener came to water the plants, Malak called to him for help. The gardener let her down with a ladder.

"What were you doing in the apricot tree?"
he asked.

"Well," said Malak, looking very contrite. "There I was, going home,
when suddenly a terrible breeze lifted me and blew me up the tree."

"Why is there apricot juice on your hands and face?"

"That's from when I held onto the branches to stop the wind from
blowing me away."

"What about the apricots in your pockets?"

"Funny you should ask," she said, looking surprised. "I was won-
dering that myself. Strange, the tricks the wind can play."

..

⬬ *The wit of the mischievous should be a warning to the wise.* ⬬

Mehallabeyat Qamaruddin (Apricot Pudding)

Qamaruddin is sheets of dried apricots, sometimes called apricot leather. It is often sold in Middle Eastern grocery stores wrapped in orange cellophane, and online under the unwieldy name Dried Apricot Fruit Paste Sheets. The sheets can be soaked or dissolved in simmering water to make a refreshing apricot drink, served chilled. Qamaruddin can also be made into a pudding, which has a consistency a little like *blancmange* or custard pudding.

SERVES 3-6

INGREDIENTS

2 sheets of dried apricot leather, approximately 8 by 10 inches, torn into strips

1 cup hot water

2 tablespoons sugar, or to taste

2 tablespoons cornstarch

To Decorate

2 teaspoons shredded coconut

2 teaspoons ground pistachios

½ cup raisins

PREPARATION

1. Put the apricot strips in a mixing bowl and cover with the hot water. Set aside to soak for 1 hour. Then pour the strips, with their liquid, into a blender and blend until smooth.

2. Set a sieve over a saucepan and strain the apricot liquid to remove any solid pieces. Put the pan over low heat and bring to a simmer. Add the sugar and cornstarch and simmer, stirring constantly, until the mixture thickens to the consistency of pudding, 5 to 10 minutes.

3. Pour the pudding into serving cups or bowls and set them aside to cool. Refrigerate until cold. Decorate with the shredded coconut, pistachios and raisins just before serving.

Qamaruddin (Apricot Sheets)

Making fruit leather is the traditional Arab way of preserving fruit. It is both fun and easy to do, though it takes time. Apricots are the most popular fruit used in fruit leather, but you can use other soft fruit, such as peaches or plums. You can even try apples, pears, figs, cherries or almost any fruit that cooks down well.

INGREDIENTS

5 cups chopped fresh apricots or other fruits (if using apples or pears, peel them first)

½ cup water

1 tablespoon sugar, or to taste

½ teaspoon cinnamon or nutmeg, if using apples and pears

2 tablespoons freshly squeezed lemon juice

PREPARATION

1. Place the fruit and water in a pot and simmer gently on low heat for 10 minutes.

2. Add the sugar, cinnamon or nutmeg (if using), and lemon juice, and continue to simmer for another 10 minutes or until the fruit breaks down and thickens.

3. Use a blender or food processor to purée the fruit until smooth.

4. If you have a food dehydrator, pour a thin (⅛-inch) layer of puréed fruit into the tray and dehydrate until dry. This may take up to 9 hours—follow the directions on your machine and check on it after 6 hours.

Alternatively, preheat the oven to 150°F and line a baking pan with aluminum foil or parchment paper. Pour a thin (⅛-inch) layer of puréed fruit into the pan and put it in the oven for up to 9 hours. Start checking on it after 7 hours—the surface should feel smooth but not sticky.

5. Once ready, remove from the dehydrator or oven and leave to cool. The fruit leather can be rolled or folded on parchment paper and stored in an airtight container in the refrigerator or freezer.

APRICOT DRINK

The English word "apricot" comes from the Arabic *al-barqouq*. The Arabs originally imported apricots from Tus in Iran and also from China (where they were first grown). Apricots are used in both sweet and savory dishes. They are also sun-dried and prepared as fruit leather (see page 18). The best apricots for qamaruddin are grown in Syria. The fruit is simmered and strained through wooden strainers that have been soaked in olive oil, then left to dry in the sun and pressed into sheets. The sheets of dried apricot can be torn into strips and soaked in rose water with dried fruits and served with nuts to make a drink also called qamaruddin. This drink is popular during the festive seasons of Eid and Easter.

DOKKA: APRICOT KERNELS

In Egypt, apricot kernels are ground and mixed with coriander seeds and salt to make a traditional snack called *dokka*. The oil from the pressed seeds is used in cooking and as a cosmetic to soothe dry skin.

The Lion Repents

One day, on a day much like today, an old lion tired of the chase and the hunt. He decided to change his ways. He called a meeting of all the animals at a place they knew as the hollow mountain. The animals came to the meeting place, but cautiously kept their distance from the lion they all feared.

The lion had combed his furry mane into a beard around his face and flattened it along his back. He appeared sad and meek, and not at all like the dreadful beast the other animals took him for. Lion spoke, in a voice so quiet the animals had to strain to hear him. After much thinking and heart-searching, Lion told them, he had come to realize that his hunting had caused much suffering in the animal kingdom. He had deprived doe and deer of parents, gazelles of their young, cows and buffaloes of their calves. What he had done to satisfy his past hunger was a sin beyond forgiveness. Tears welled in the lion's eyes. He wiped them from his cheeks with the back of his furry paw. Weighed down by terrible guilt, Lion declared, he had decided he would no longer eat flesh. From now on he would only eat berries, fruit fallen from trees, and root vegetables when in season. Lion pleaded for the other animals to excuse his past mistakes, but said he knew that total forgiveness was not possible.

"If you can find it in your hearts," he added, "please pray I may find the strength to rid myself of the evil that has led me to live a wicked life." With these words, Lion withdrew into his cave to make amends, he said, for his sins.

"Who would have thought such a thing possible?" said the rabbit. "The lion has gained wisdom beyond words."

"To recognize one's faults is a sign of true greatness," agreed the hedgehog.

"If only we could all learn such humility," mumbled the buffalo as he munched on a prickly shrub.

"His teeth and claws look much the same today as they did before," said Hamdan the baboon.

"Be fair," squawked the peacock. "Every animal deserves a second chance."

"An awakening," declared the flamingo. "He is woke. Woke, I tell you."

"Well put," guffawed the hyena, scratching his belly with his paw.

The lion came out of his cave and said the animals should go to their homes, knowing they were safe forever. He hung his head low and returned to the darkness of the hollow mountain.

The other animals continued their praise of the lion reborn as a lamb.

"He should be encouraged," cackled the hens.

"Yes, yes, I do declare." The ass beat its hooves on the dusty ground.

"Who among us volunteers to go to him to offer our encouragement?" sniggered the hyena.

"He will hear it first from me," announced the buffalo. "I will be your messenger."

"The lion should know forgiveness is always possible," said the hare, raising clouds of dust as it applauded the buffalo by beating its

hind legs on the ground.

"Hee-haw!" agreed the wild ass.

"Caution is a virtue worth cultivating," said Hamdan the baboon, but none of the animals were listening. They cheered the buffalo for being the bearer of forgiveness.

The buffalo bobbed his head back and forth, acknowledging the praise of the animal herds and flocks. Indeed, he felt he was on the path to sainthood as he crossed from the sunlight of the clearing into the shadows of the lion's den.

The animals waited and waited for the buffalo to return. The light began to fade and the sun to set. They started to clamor for the buffalo to show itself. It was dusk before the lion appeared. With a smile of contentment, Lion told the crowd of animals he had a message for them.

"My dear friend, Buffalo, has agreed to stay a while to offer me the benefit of his worldly wisdom. Maybe in a week or two some of you may want to join us."

The animals applauded Lion and cheered Buffalo for his kindness.

Hamdan the baboon said they should not trust the lion, for a cat may live in a monastery but will still hunt mice. And why hadn't Buffalo spoken for himself, instead of leaving the talking to Lion? But the other animals ignored the baboon and made their way home to lairs and nests. In the failing light, they chatted about who among them would be next to visit the lion and show him forgiveness. The wild ass argued with the hens, saying he would be next.

"Cluck, cluck," retorted the hens. They would be next. "Just you wait and see."

26

Alone, Hamdan the baboon returned to the crevice in the stone hill that was his home. He felt sorry for Buffalo and all who would follow him.

..

❧ *More have suffered by trust than vigilance.* ❧

Fattoush (Zesty Salad)

This simple salad is popular all over the Arab world. It is usually topped with crispy pita bread. *Fattoush* goes well with grilled lamb and chicken dishes.

SERVES 2-4

INGREDIENTS

1 head of Romaine lettuce, washed and chopped

2 tomatoes, diced

2 Persian or Lebanese cucumbers, diced

6 scallions, sliced

1 pita bread

Dressing

2 tablespoons extra-virgin olive oil

juice of 1 lemon

¼ teaspoon salt

1 teaspoon sumac

Topping

2 tablespoons chopped parsley

10 fresh mint leaves, coarsely chopped

PREPARATION

1. In a large salad bowl, mix together the lettuce, tomatoes, cucumbers and scallions.

2. Toast the pita bread in your toaster or oven until it is brown and crispy—watch carefully so it doesn't burn. Break the toasted pita bread into bite-sized pieces and mix into the salad.

3. Make the dressing by mixing the olive oil, lemon juice, salt and sumac. Pour the dressing over the salad and toss to coat everything well.

4. Sprinkle with the chopped mint and parsley, then serve.

VARYING YOUR SALAD

Though toasted or fried pita bread is traditional, you can use bread croutons. You can also add 4 or 5 coarsely chopped fresh basil leaves or a handful of dill along with the mint. The salad can also be served with crumbled feta cheese, black olives, chives and capers. For a stronger flavor, use finely chopped red onion instead of the scallions and jazz up the dressing with a tablespoon of pomegranate molasses. Sumac adds a pleasing dash of red to the salad.

MEZZE MUNCHIES

In Arabic, the word *mezze* means "to taste," with the implication that what is being tasted is tasty. The word is most commonly applied to the small dishes served as appetizers before a main meal or as an evening snack. These can be small salads such as fattoush and tabouli (pages 28 and 62), olives, slices of cheese, a yogurt dip (*lebne*), hummus (page 36), baba ghanoush (page 78), vegetables or pickles and maybe small meat or seafood dishes. The dishes are shared and are meant to encourage conversation.

WHAT IS SUMAC?

Sumac is a dark red berry related to the cashew nut. It grows on bushes native to the Middle East. It is dried and ground to produce a spice with a bold, tart citrus flavor. It can also be purchased as dried berries and as juice. Sumac is a popular ingredient in Arab cuisine. It is most commonly used to flavor fattoush and chicken dishes, and as a key ingredient in *zaatar*, a blend of herbs and spices (page 48). Sumac can also be mixed with plain yogurt as a delicious side dish or dip.

31

The Story and the Chickpeas

Once, long ago, there lived a little girl who was much like you and me when we were her age. Her name was Salwa and she lived in a city called Sanaa, in Yemen. Salwa had a story to tell, but wouldn't tell it to anyone.

At night, while Salwa slept, the story would say it needed to be told. The little girl would refuse. The story would get all choked up and angry. It demanded to be told. After all, stories are for telling. It gave Salwa all sorts of bad dreams, but still she would not tell anyone, not even her mother.

Some evenings, her mother would ask Salwa to prepare chickpeas for cooking the next day. The girl would rinse them, then leave them to soak overnight, ready to be boiled the next morning. On one such night, while everybody slept, the story crept out of the girl. It went to the pot and tipped it over. The next morning, the girl's mother scolded her for spilling the chickpeas all over the kitchen floor.

"I didn't do it," Salwa said. "Honest, it wasn't me."

Her mother told her to rinse the chickpeas and put them back in the pot to soak. That night, the story again slipped out while Salwa slept and knocked the pot over. Once more, the little girl was scolded and had to rinse and soak the chickpeas. The next night, the story tipped the pot over again. But this time, Salwa was pretending to be asleep and saw what happened. It was then Salwa knew she would never get any peace until the story had been told. She cleared up the mess the story had made and put the chickpeas back in the pot to soak. Then she woke her mother and told her the story and how troublesome it had been because it wanted to be told.

When Salwa went back to bed, she slept the best sleep she'd had in weeks. The next morning, her mother simmered the chickpeas on the stove and cooked a tasty meal of them.

∷

Even a secret fire must give off smoke.

Hummus bil Laban (Hummus and Yogurt Layered Dip)

If anything calls to mind Arab cooking, it is hummus, which is also the Arabic word for chickpeas. Hummus can be served as a dip with pita bread or vegetables, as a delicious appetizer, or as a side dish. In this recipe, it is layered with garlicky yogurt. You can leave out the yogurt layer, if you like, and just use half the amount of toasted bread.

SERVES 4

INGREDIENTS

Hummus

28 oz can of chickpeas, drained and rinsed (about 3 cups)

4 tablespoons tahini (sesame paste), or to taste

½ cup freshly squeezed lemon juice, or to taste

4 garlic cloves, minced, or to taste

¼ teaspoon salt, or to taste

Layers

1 cup plain Greek yogurt

2 garlic cloves, minced, or to taste

3 pita breads, plus extra for serving

Topping

½ cup pine nuts

½ cup chopped parsley

1 tablespoon sumac

2 tablespoons extra-virgin olive oil, plus extra for drizzling

PREPARATION

For the Hummus

Set aside ½ cup of the chickpeas to decorate the hummus. Place the remaining chickpeas in a food processor and add the tahini, lemon juice, garlic and salt. Blend until you have a smooth paste. Taste and blend in more salt, lemon juice, garlic or tahini if you like.

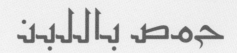

For the Layers

1. In a small bowl, mix the yogurt and garlic. Set aside.

2. Toast the pita bread in your toaster or oven until it is brown and crispy—watch carefully so it doesn't burn. Break the toasted pita bread into bite-sized pieces.

3. In a small frying pan, heat the oil over medium heat and fry the pine nuts until golden brown. Watch carefully because they can burn easily. Set aside.

4. Now you are ready to make your layers: Spoon half of the hummus into a large, shallow serving bowl and scatter half of the crispy bread on this layer. Spoon the garlicky yogurt on top, sprinkle with the rest of the crispy pita bread, and top with the rest of the hummus.

5. Decorate the top with the leftover chickpeas, fried nuts, chopped parsley and a sprinkle of sumac. Serve with pita bread on the side.

Muhammas (Crispy Chickpeas)

Traditionally, instead of snacking on popcorn, kids in the Middle East munch on roasted, crispy chickpeas. These are often sold, warm and spiced, in paper cones by street-side vendors and at fairgrounds.

SERVES 2-4

INGREDIENTS

28 oz can of chickpeas, drained and rinsed (about 3 cups)

2 tablespoons extra-virgin olive oil

1 teaspoon salt

2 tablespoons of your favorite ground spices like curry powder, cumin and paprika.

PREPARATION

1. Preheat the oven to 375°F.

2. Place the chickpeas in a baking pan. In a small bowl, mix the salt and olive oil and pour over the chickpeas, stirring them until they are fully coated in oil. Spread the chickpeas out evenly in the pan.

3. Roast the chickpeas until they are golden brown, 20 to 30 minutes. They should be crispy on the outside and soft inside.

4. Remove from the oven and toss in the spices, mixing to coat them well. Serve warm.

A PEA WITH A HISTORY

Chickpeas have been found in a number of ancient sites in the Middle East—some 7,500 years old—from Egypt to Mesopotamia (modern-day Iraq). The earliest evidence of chickpeas being grown is in Syria. The famous thirteenth-century poet Jalaluddin Rumi wrote a number of short stories in praise of the chickpea. He considered it an everyman kind of legume: simple and straightforward, but also versatile and nourishing.

A Pot of Coins

They say, or so they said, many years ago in a district of old Cairo in Egypt, there lived a miser called Muhsin. Muhsin had long ago decided to give up working for a living. Instead, he spent his days sitting on the corner of a street, begging for alms. He put the coins he collected in a clay pot and hid it on the roof of the house where he lived. To avoid spending his loot, he would beg storekeepers for bread and whatever vegetables were in season. Some days, he would be given a cup or two of lentils to make himself some soup. Other days, he might bring home flour and salt and a pinch or two of mixed herbs to bake zaatar flatbread.

On his way to and from the mosque, Muhsin would pass a group of children playing soccer with a ball made from rags tightly wound together. He would scowl at them, and they would tease him, asking for money. He would yell at the girls and boys to get out of his way, swearing and cussing in a most unfriendly way.

In the evenings, he would climb the stairs to his rooftop hiding place and remove his hoard of coins. He'd run his fingers through the coins as though in greeting, and they would make a wonderful clinking sound like tiny bells. He thought they must be aware of him, as he was aware of each one of them. Dark or light in color, some were rubbed smooth in places while others were like new. The faces on the coins, it seemed, were of old friends he had long known, each having survived life's trials to find a home in his pot of coins. He fingered them, counted them, spoke to them as companions and imagined what he would one day do with his wealth. He could see himself living in a great house on an island in the Nile, with servants he would order to do this and that and bring him whatever he wanted. On the grounds would be a stable for the finest Arabian stallions, cared for by stable hands who obeyed his every word. Young princes and princesses would arrive from near and far wanting to meet him, the man of legendary riches and refined taste.

One evening, he sat with his hoard of coins in front of him and watched the boys and girls playing in the street. He imagined, once he was rich, what he would do to those pesky kids. He would have his servants chase them away. Oh yes, he could picture the scene. He swung an arm up in the air, as though shooing the brats away, and— "Oh no!"—he sent the pot flying from the rooftop. The pot fell and fell, smashing to the ground, scattering its clinking coins. Muhsin the Miser watched as the children in the street rushed with glee to gather his fallen treasure.

••

He who dreams only of tomorrow will never see tomorrow come.

Shorbit Adas (Simple Lentil Soup)

Soups are popular all over the Arab world, from spicy North African *harira* (a hearty meat and legume soup) to mild Lebanese *labaneya* (a kind of yogurt soup). Below is a simple recipe for delicious lentil soup. Spinach or chopped cilantro are often added in the final stages of making the soup.

SERVES 4–6

INGREDIENTS

6 tablespoons extra-virgin olive oil

1 onion, finely chopped

1½ cups red lentils, rinsed

1 teaspoon ground cumin

½ teaspoon ground white pepper

6 cups water or chicken stock

2–4 garlic cloves, minced

1 teaspoon salt, or to taste

To serve (optional)

handful of chopped parsley or cilantro

croutons or toasted and flaked pita bread

lemon wedges

PREPARATION

1. In a soup pot, heat 4 tablespoons of the olive oil and sauté the onion over low heat until translucent, 5 to 10 minutes.

2. Add the lentils, cumin and white pepper and cook, stirring, until the lentils begin to turn yellow, about 5 minutes.

3. Add the water or stock and bring to a boil, then turn down the heat, cover and simmer for 30 to 45 minutes, or until the lentils are very soft and mushy.

4. In a small frying pan, heat the remaining 2 tablespoons of olive oil over medium heat and sauté the garlic until golden, then stir it into the soup. Simmer the soup, stirring occasionally, for 10 more minutes. Mix in the salt.

5. Serve in soup bowls, topped with parsley or cilantro and the croutons, with lemon wedges on the side for squeezing.

Manakish Zaatar (Zaatar Flatbread)

Zaatar is a blend of herbs and spices, usually made up of dried wild thyme, sumac and sesame seeds, though other ingredients are added in different parts of the Middle East. It can be purchased from Middle Eastern grocery stores and online (see page 48 to make your own). The following recipe is for flatbread, but you can also roll the dough into equal-length ropes, then roll the ropes in the zaatar mixture and bake as breadsticks. You can also use store-bought pizza dough as a shortcut (just be sure to follow the instructions on the package).

SERVES 4

INGREDIENTS

Dough

1 teaspoon active-dry yeast

½ teaspoon sugar

1 cup warm water

2 cups all-purpose flour, plus extra for dusting

1 teaspoon salt

3 tablespoons extra-virgin olive oil, plus extra for greasing

Topping

6 tablespoons extra-virgin olive oil

5–6 tablespoons zaatar

PREPARATION

1. In a small bowl, combine the yeast, sugar and ½ cup of the warm water and set aside for 5 to 10 minutes until frothy.

2. In a mixing bowl, mix the flour and salt together. Make a well in the middle and pour in the yeast mixture, olive oil and the remaining ½ cup of warm water and gradually stir until you have a shaggy dough. Tip the dough out onto

a lightly floured work surface and knead for 10 minutes until smooth and elastic. Place the dough in a lightly oiled bowl, cover with a clean kitchen towel and set aside in a warm place to rise until doubled in size, about 1 hour.

3. Cut the dough into 4 equal pieces, roll into smooth balls, cover with the towel and set aside for a final 5 to 10 minutes.

4. Preheat the oven to 400°F. Lightly oil a baking pan (or you can use a pizza stone if you have one). Flatten the dough into 3- to 5-inch rounds, each about ½-inch thick, and place on the greased baking pan.

5. Make the topping: in a small bowl, mix the olive oil and zaatar and spread it over the flattened dough rounds.

6. Bake until the dough is cooked and golden, 7 to 10 minutes.

7. The flatbread can be served with sliced tomatoes, cucumbers, feta cheese and olives.

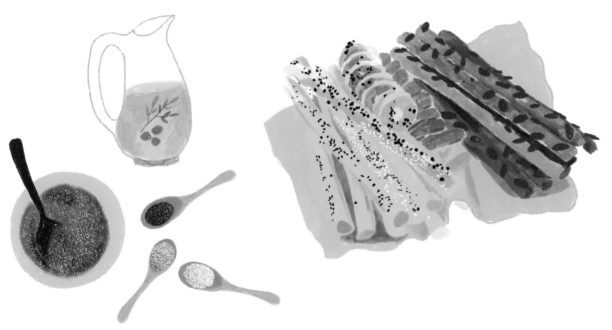

MAKE YOUR OWN ZAATAR

This spice and herb blend is easy enough to make. Combine a tablespoon each of crushed dried thyme or oregano, toasted sesame seeds and ground sumac, and add a pinch of salt to taste. You can add a tablespoon of ground cumin and ground coriander, too, and if you like it hot, you can add a pinch of red pepper flakes. Mix well, and there you have it.

AN ANCIENT LEGUME

The word "lentil" comes from the Latin word for lens, like the glass in a pair of spectacles. The Arabic word also means lens. This seems to be a case of Arabic borrowing a word from Latin, but it is more likely the name comes from an ancient language called Aramaic. This language is older than either Arabic or Latin and was once spoken throughout the Middle East. All this goes to show that lentils have been around for a long time. They are even mentioned in the Bible and they remain a popular and nutritious food today.

SESAME SEEDS

The use of sesame in cooking and medicine has a long history. It was first grown in the Bronze Age in Mesopotamia, which today is Iraq. Sesame was also grown in ancient Egypt and seeds were found in the pharaoh Tutankhamen's tomb. In the tale of Ali Baba from *The Thousand and One Nights* (also called *The Arabian Nights*), sesame is famously the word that opens the cave where the forty thieves hid their treasure. It is also the answer to a children's rhyming riddle in Arabic: "What is nourishing if you eat all of it, but eating half of it will kill you?" To answer the riddle, you need to know that the Arabic word for sesame is *simsim* and the word for poison is a single *sim*.

Fish Soup in Gaza

In days of yore and times long gone before, on the Gaza waterfront in Palestine, between the wharf and Beach Camp, old man Goha told Fadia, his granddaughter, of the days when the sea was full of fish. On one such day, he said, he went fishing and caught the largest fish ever seen by man or beast.

"It started off with me catching a fish the size of your teeny tiny finger. I decided to leave the fish on the hook and cast the line again. Immediately, I felt a tug on the line and reeled in the catch. It was a fish the size of your hand. I left the fish on the line and cast again and, lo and behold, there was an even stronger tug. When I reeled in the line, I saw I'd caught a fish the very size of you from head to toe. Leaving the fish on the hook, I cast the line again. This time the tug was so strong it nearly lifted me off the wharf. With great effort, I reeled it in to see a fish the size of a camel. Deciding to chance it, I cast the line with the great fish. Before I could catch my breath, there was a pull that nearly wrenched the wharf off its foundation. With the help of some boys and girls on the beach, I was able to draw in the line to see I'd caught a fish the size of an ocean liner. I decided then I had no more strength to continue fishing. Do you know, that fish fed everybody at Beach Camp for a month? With the bones, we made fish soup that lasted us a whole year."

"Do you know, Grandfather, just the other week I was at the ceramics center in Khan Yunis," Fadia said. "The potters told me they had built the greatest kiln you've ever seen in which they fired a pot three times the size of the al-Aqsa mosque in Jerusalem."

"That's ridiculous," Goha huffed.

"Well, it must be true," Fadia replied. "You see, they were the potters who made the pot in which you cooked that fish you caught."

..

It can take a lie to expose a lie so the truth may be known.

Hassa al-Samak (Fish Soup)

All Arab countries border seas and oceans, and several have rivers cutting through them. So, it can hardly be a surprise that fish soups and broths are popular. This recipe uses spicy Moroccan *harissa* sauce, which you can find online or from Middle Eastern grocery stores, but if you don't like spicy foods, leave it out.

SERVES 4

INGREDIENTS

12 oz skinless white fish fillets like cod or haddock

1 teaspoon salt

1 teaspoon ground black pepper

2 teaspoons ground cumin

juice of 1 lemon

½ cup all-purpose flour

¼ cup extra-virgin olive oil

½ onion, chopped

1 teaspoon ground coriander

4 garlic cloves, minced

2 tomatoes, diced

1 potato, diced

1 carrot

1 teaspoon tomato paste

1 tablespoon red harissa sauce (optional)

3 cups fish stock

2 bay leaves

4 cardamom pods

Garnish

lemon slices

chopped cilantro

PREPARATION

1. Sprinkle the fish fillets with the salt, pepper, cumin and the juice of 1 lemon. Put the flour in a shallow dish and coat the fillets in flour, shaking off excess. Set aside.

2. In a soup pot, heat the oil over medium heat. When the oil is hot, place the fish fillets in the pot and cook for about 5 minutes on each side until seared. Remove the fish from the pot and set aside.

3. In the same pot, sauté the onion over medium-low heat until translucent, 5 to 10 minutes. Add the ground coriander and stir over low heat for about 1 minute. Add the garlic, tomatoes, potato and carrot. Stir in the tomato paste and harissa (if using).

4. Pour in the fish stock, making sure it covers the ingredients in the pot (top up with water, if needed) and add the bay leaves and cardamom pods. Bring to a boil, then turn down the heat and simmer, covered, until the vegetables are very soft, about 30 minutes. Return the fish to the pot and continue to simmer for 3 to 5 minutes more until the fish is cooked through.

5. Remove the bay leaves and cardamom pods. Carefully transfer the soup to a blender or food processor or use a handheld stick blender to blend until smooth.

6. Serve in soup bowls topped with chopped cilantro, with lemon slices on the side for squeezing.

HARISSA SAUCE

Harissa sauce comes in two varieties: green and red. The red is a mixture of hot chilies and red peppers with ground coriander and cumin seeds, garlic and lemon—all blended to make a distinctively flavored hot sauce. Green harissa replaces some of the peppers with scallions and cilantro to give the sauce a milder flavor.

WHO WAS GOHA (JOHA)?

Goha, sometimes spelled Joha, is a wise fool who appears in many children's tales told throughout the Arab world. In many of these stories his most common companion is his donkey. The real-life inspiration for these stories was a man with a mouthful of a name, Abu al-Ghusn Dajin al-Fazari, who lived in the seventh century. His home was the city of Kufa, in present-day Iraq. The earliest published collections of Goha stories are from the tenth century.

Another real person who inspired Goha stories was a man named Nasruddin Hodja who lived in Konya, in present-day Turkey. The poet Rumi mocked him by calling him Goha and the association stuck. Although Nasruddin died in the thirteenth century, many of the stories pit him against the sultan Tamburlaine the Great who lived in the fourteenth century and involve him outwitting the harsh and unkindly king.

Goha stories have crossed the Mediterranean to Sicily and southern Italy. There, he is known in Italian folklore as Giufà. In these tales, rather than struggling with a stubborn donkey, he often has to deal with a bossy mother. Goha may even have been the inspiration for the wonderful Spanish novel *Don Quixote*, written by Miguel de Cervantes and published over 400 years ago.

Abu Nawas Tells a Tale

Abu Nawas had a falling out with his wife. He never had any money for her to spend on their home. They argued and she threw him out, telling him never to show his face again. She wouldn't let him collect any of his belongings or fetch his wallet. He wandered through the city streets, feeling sad and growing hungrier and hungrier. It was sunset and the streets were emptying of people returning home for their evening meal. He tried begging at a mosque, but nobody gave him any money. "You're all charlatans," he shouted and continued on his way. He stopped by a house close to the military barracks and asked the lady of the house for something to eat.

She seemed surprised to see a man so well dressed in such a fine *abaya* (cloak) and turban begging at her door. "Where did you come from?" she asked.

"From the pits of Hell, I can tell you," he replied.

She invited him into the house. She poured him a chilled pomegranate drink and ordered the servants to provide him with a meal of roast meat and vegetables, salads and sweet desserts.

"When you were in Hell, did you see my son Burhan?" she asked.

"If he was there, I would have seen him," Abu Nawas muttered as he tucked into a bowl of tabouli.

"I knew he'd end up there." The woman screamed and wailed. "A mother's intuition never fails. Is my child in pain?"

"For sure, Hell is pain," said Abu Nawas as he kept eating, not thinking much about the conversation.

When Abu Nawas had finished the meal, she asked him if he would be returning to Hell. "I should think so," he said. "I don't have anywhere else to go."

"Does having some money help in a place like Hell?"

"It's the only thing that does." Abu Nawas shrugged, thinking of his wife.

The woman opened her purse and handed Abu Nawas a bunch of gold coins. "Please, do a grieving mother a favor. When you get there, I beg you to search out my son and give him these dinars."

Abu Nawas took the coins and promised to do his best to find her son. He left the woman, not believing his luck, and headed home.

Shortly after, the woman's husband returned. He was an officer in the sultan's cavalry. No sooner had he dismounted from his horse than he saw his wife crying.

"What's wrong?" he asked.

"A man who's seen our son in Hell just came by the house. I gave him some money to give to the boy."

The officer flew into a temper. "You don't just come and go from Hell. Where is the crook?" His wife pointed in the direction Abu Nawas had gone.

The officer got back on his horse and rode down the road at a gallop.

Abu Nawas, with a full belly, had made slow progress. He stopped by the mosque to drink at a water fountain when he saw the officer on his horse.

"Have you seen a charlatan who claims to have arrived from Hell?" asked the officer.

"A charlatan, you say," said Abu Nawas. "For sure he'll be in the mosque."

The officer jumped off his horse and rushed in. Abu Nawas mounted the horse and rode off.

The officer returned home on foot.

"Where's the horse?" his wife asked.

"I sent it to Hell so our son would have something to ride when he pays off the devil," he growled at her.

Back home, Abu Nawas gave his wife the gold coins, which sweetened her mood.

"Where'd you get such a fine horse?" she asked.

"I was given it to go to Hell."

"Welcome home," she said.

∴

It's a foolish lamb that seeks the help of the wolf.

Tabouli (Parsley and Bulgur Salad)

Tabouli can be served as a mezze (or a tasty nibble) alongside hummus (page 36), baba ghanoush (page 78), fattoush (page 28) and lamb kofta (page 80), or it can be an appetizer or side dish. The name comes from the Arabic *tawabil*, meaning spices. This may seem a little odd given how few spices are actually used in preparing tabouli. But not so strange if you consider the original meaning of tawabil was "seeds." This was likely a reference to the grains of bulgur, a grain derived from wheat.

SERVES 4

INGREDIENTS

½ cup fine bulgur

¾ cup warm water

4 Lebanese or Persian cucumbers, diced (optional)

3 tomatoes, diced

1 teaspoon salt, or to taste

2 cups parsley, finely chopped

⅓ cup fresh mint, finely chopped

⅓ cup finely sliced scallions

Dressing

⅓ cup extra-virgin olive oil

3 tablespoons freshly squeezed lemon juice, or to taste

1 garlic clove, minced

PREPARATION

1. Soak the bulgur in the warm water until soft, 20 to 30 minutes. Drain the water and place the bulgur in a large serving bowl.

2. In a separate bowl, sprinkle the cucumbers and tomatoes with ½ teaspoon of the salt. Mix well and set aside for 15 minutes, then pour off the liquid. (You can skip this step if you like your tabouli moist.)

3. Add the tomatoes, cucumbers, parsley, mint and scallions to the bulgur in the serving bowl and toss to mix.

4. In another bowl or cup, make the dressing by whisking together the olive oil, lemon juice, garlic and the remaining ½ teaspoon of salt.

5. Add the dressing to the salad and toss to mix well. Taste and add more lemon juice or salt if needed.

Pomegranate Spritz

Pomegranates make a delicious drink. In many parts of the Arab world, you can buy freshly prepared pomegranate juice from street vendors. If you buy yours in a bottle, remember the juice may discolor soon once opened because of its high iron content, so be sure to store it in a sealed container in the refrigerator.

SERVES 1-2

INGREDIENTS

1 cup pomegranate juice

1 cup sparkling water, club soda or lime-flavored soda

1 teaspoon of sugar, or to taste (skip if using sweetened juice or soda)

crushed ice, to serve

PREPARATION

1. Combine the pomegranate juice and sparkling water or soda in a pitcher, and stir. Taste and add sugar until the spritz is sweetened to your liking.

2. Put the ice into a glass or glasses, pour in the spritz and serve.

عصير الرمان

ABU NAWAS: THE POET TRICKSTER

Abu Nawas was a famous ninth-century Arab poet who gained
a reputation for lavish living that caused him to become a
popular character in folk tales. He lived at the time of the
legendary Caliph Harun al-Rashid, who ruled a large empire.
It spanned from the shores of the Atlantic Ocean in the west
to the borders of China in the east. The city of Baghdad was
its capital. This was also the time and location of many of the
fantastical tales in *The Thousand and One Nights*, several of
which are about Abu Nawas and Harun al-Rashid.

THE FRUIT OF HEAVEN

In much of the Middle East, the pomegranate is a symbol of
plenty. Some people believe pomegranate trees, along with olive,
date and fig trees, are the four earthly trees that will be found
in Heaven. Among some, it is believed that a pomegranate,
rather than an apple, was the forbidden fruit Adam and Eve
tasted in paradise. In some places, the fruit is served to a bride
on her wedding day to bless her so she will have many children.
Also, for that same reason, the fruit is sometimes split at her
feet, scattering its seeds.

Why Chicken and Ostrich Cannot Fly

At a time long before you and I were born, along the Sahel plains at the edge of the Sahara Desert, it was said all birds could fly. In those days, Chicken and Ostrich were the best of friends. They were always in each other's company; you never saw one without the other. Then came a long dry summer—the worst heat and drought any of the birds in the plains had ever known. The birds held a meeting to decide what to do. Once together, they chittered and chirped. But, as much as they talked in bird chatter, they could not agree on a solution. Finally, the wise old African openbill stork came forward and said, "As we cannot decide among ourselves, we must seek the advice of another."

The kite and the goose were first to agree and gradually the flamingo, ostrich, ibis and spoonbill gave their support. Eventually even the ducks and herons saw the sense of what the stork had proposed. Soon all the birds were in agreement. Yes indeed, they would need to consult one wiser than themselves.

"But who should we go to?" asked the shoebill.

"The wisest of the wise," said the eagle, "is none other than the salamander who lives in the woodlands by the great river."

They had all heard of the fire salamander, her skin black with flame-like speckles of red. Her magical powers were known. Her knowledge of poisons was feared.

Late that night, the birds all fluttered
and flew to the edge of the river where the
fire salamander lived. They approached her lair
with caution and waited for her to appear. Once the
moon shone in its fullness, the salamander came out
of her lair from the side of a fallen tree. The raven explained
their plight. "Oh wise salamander, what is to be done?"

"Nothing forfeit, nothing gained," hissed the salamander. "You
must each give me a feather for my nest. Then I will tell you what
you can do to save yourselves from this heat and drought."

One after another, each bird plucked a feather from tail or wing
and laid it before the salamander. When it came to Ostrich's turn,
Ostrich said, preening herself, "My feathers are the prettiest and the
finest. One feather of mine is worth more than all those feathers put
together."

"My advice is worth your feather," murmured the salamander,
flicking her tongue.

Prancing on her two feet, twirling to show off the long white
plumes on her wings and tail, Ostrich said, "I'll think about it."

"I, too, have pretty feathers," said
Chicken, skipping from one foot to the
other. "If Ostrich won't give a feather, then neither will I."
To one group of birds, the salamander said, "You must fly
north to the delta where the great river meets the sea." To another
she said, "Fly east to the Zagros Mountains," and to yet another,
"Fly west, to the Atlas Mountains." There, the salamander said, the
birds would find the air cool and moist and to their liking.

With first light, the birds rose and spread their wings. Some flew
north, others east and some flew west. The ostrich and the chicken
waited until last. When they came to flap their wings, nothing happened. They flapped and flapped, but could not lift themselves into
the air. They ran and flapped, and flapped and ran, but try as they
might they could not fly.

Ever since, the ostrich and the chicken, too proud to give a feather
to the salamander, have not been able to fly.

••

When pride blossoms, folly is its fruit.

Shish Taouk (Chicken Kebab)

The popularity and availability of the kebab means it needs little introduction. I have no wish to offend the national pride of Persians, Turks, Amazigh, Kurds, Armenians or Arabs who all claim first rights over the kebab. Therefore, I will not venture into a discussion about the kebab's possible origins. For this recipe you will need about eight 6-inch wooden skewers, soaked in water for 15 minutes before use.

SERVES 2–4

INGREDIENTS

2 boneless, skinless chicken breasts, cut into 2-inch cubes

2 bell peppers

1 onion

Marinade

½ cup plain yogurt

½ cup freshly squeezed lemon juice

½ cup extra-virgin olive oil

2 garlic cloves, minced

1 teaspoon ground nutmeg

1 teaspoon ground cardamom

2 teaspoons salt

1 teaspoon ground black pepper

PREPARATION

1. In a large mixing bowl, mix the marinade ingredients together well. Add the chicken pieces and stir to coat them in the marinade. Refrigerate for at least 2 hours to marinate.

2. Cut the bell peppers and onion into chunks roughly the same size as the chicken cubes.

3. Thread onto skewers, alternating pieces of chicken, peppers and onions. Be careful not to pack them too tightly.

4. Preheat your grill or place the skewers on an oven rack. Grill or broil for 10 to 15 minutes, turning them over once, until cooked through.

5. Serve with rice, couscous or pita bread, and side dishes like hummus (page 36), baba ghanoush (page 78) and fattoush (page 28).

BREAD IS LIFE

Though flatbreads like pita are commonly associated with Arab countries, there are many other types of traditional bread. These include fried *sfinz*, the pancake-like *shebab*, crunchy folded *malawah*, the thin-sheeted *saj* and *regag*, pocket-like *khubz arabi* and *shami* as well as the thick bread loaves of the Levant. The standard Arabic word for bread is *khobz*, but in many places it is called *aysh*, which means life.

THE FIRE SALAMANDER

The fire salamander was once common to the Eastern Mediterranean. It lives close to rivers and springs. Its black body has fiery orange and yellow patches. In ancient times, it was believed the fire salamander could spit powerful poisons and had the magical power to both extinguish fire and regenerate itself in the flames, like the mythical Phoenix. Unfortunately for the salamander, none of these superpowers were real, and it is now an endangered species.

The Last Supper

Once, in a time unknown, and a city far from our own, there lived a merchant's widow whose name was Bashira. She was rich, and so there were many who tried to take advantage of her. They would sit in the city's coffeehouses, sip their coffee and gossip about her.

"The widow Bashira is a rich woman. I am sure she can afford to hold a dinner party that would be the talk of the town," said one of the gossips. "But she never does."

"She would probably consider it showing off in some silly way," scoffed another. They continued to sip their coffee and ponder how to fool the widow Bashira.

"What if we can convince her the world is about to end?" said the first gossip, putting aside his cup. The other gossips stopped sipping and stared at him. "We can dress up in our finest and pretend one of us is an astrologer who can read fortunes in the stars," continued the first gossip. "We'll tell her, as she must know, that on Judgement Day, the miserly will be punished for hoarding their wealth. The most pious thing she can do is spend as much of it as she can before the world ends."

"Yes, like on a feast that we can attend," said the second gossip, excited at the thought.

A third gossip agreed it was a great idea. The three gossips went home to dress in their best coats and cloaks. They hennaed their beards and wrapped their heads with their finest turbans. When they thought themselves fit in all their finery, they set off to the widow Bashira's house.

In the reception room, they talked of the mysterious ways of fate and how its signs can be read in the stars. They told the widow Bashira how the world was about to end that very night, and what she needed to do to find a place in heaven with the angels.

The widow Bashira listened politely to them. She agreed there was no time to be wasted if the world was indeed about to end. She ordered her servants to take the guests' coats and turbans, and to prepare the finest meal they could on such short notice.

The meal lasted several hours and was indeed a very fine meal. It began with an assortment of mezze, including baba ghanoush and lamb puffballs. Then came several main courses and the sweetest desserts. The gossips declared this was the best meal they had ever eaten. Then, after sipping some fine Yemeni coffee, lightly roasted and carefully brewed in a brass *ibrik*, with only an hour or so until midnight, the guests forced themselves up to leave. They said they would have to get to their homes in a hurry to prepare for the end of the world. They asked for their coats and turbans.

"You'll be pleased to know," said the widow Bashira, "I thought as, on your word, the world is about to end, the most pious thing I could do was ensure your place with me in heaven. So, I sold your coats and turbans to cover the cost of the meal." She laughed as she led the gossips, groaning, to the door.

..

A sparrow hunting for locusts may fall prey to the hawk.

Baba Ghanoush (Eggplant Dip)

Eggplant, also known as aubergine, is often made into a dip eaten as mezze with pita bread. To increase the flavor, you can mix a teaspoon of ground cumin and another of ground coriander into the dip. The dip is often decorated with olive oil and chopped parsley or cilantro.

SERVES 4

INGREDIENTS

3 large, firm eggplants with smooth skin

3 tablespoons tahini (sesame paste)

⅓ cup freshly squeezed lemon juice

2 garlic cloves

1 teaspoon ground coriander (optional)

1 teaspoon ground cumin (optional)

1 cup plain yogurt

¾ teaspoon salt, or to taste

¼ teaspoon ground black pepper

Garnish

extra-virgin olive oil

1 tablespoon pomegranate seeds (optional)

handful of mint leaves or chopped parsley or cilantro

بابا غنوج

PREPARATION

1. Preheat the oven to 375°F or turn on the broiler. Pierce the eggplants a few times with a fork. Put them on a foil-lined baking pan and broil or roast, turning them from time to time, until the insides are very soft and the skin is charred all over, 30 to 45 minutes. You can also do this on a barbecue. Remove the eggplants from the oven, cover with a clean dish towel and set aside until they are cool enough to touch.

2. Peel off the charred skin of the eggplants and put the cooked flesh into a food processor. Add the tahini, lemon juice, garlic and spices (if using), then blend to mix. Add the yogurt and blend again until smooth, then taste and add salt and pepper to your liking.

3. Place the mixture in a serving bowl. Drizzle with olive oil and decorate the top with pomegranate seeds (if using) and the mint, parsley or cilantro. Serve with pita bread as part of a mezze (page 30).

Arays Kufta (Lamb Puffballs)

These delicious bite-size pastries are filled with spiced lamb and served with a cucumber-yogurt dip. They make a great snack, and are sometimes served as part of an afternoon or evening mezze, along with hummus (page 36) and baba ghanoush (page 78).

SERVES 6

INGREDIENTS

Meatballs

1 lb ground lamb

½ cup chopped parsley

1 onion, finely chopped

3 garlic cloves, minced

¾ teaspoon salt

½ teaspoon ground black pepper

¼ teaspoon ground cumin

¼ teaspoon ground coriander

1 egg

Pastry

all-purpose flour, for dusting

2 sheets of ready-rolled puff pastry, thawed overnight in the fridge

1 egg

1 tablespoon milk

2 teaspoons water

Yogurt Dip

½ cup plain yogurt

1 Persian or Lebanese cucumber, finely chopped

1 garlic clove, minced

¼ teaspoon salt, or to taste

PREPARATION

1. In a mixing bowl, combine the lamb, parsley, onion, garlic, salt, pepper, cumin and coriander. Add the egg and mix well. Divide the mixture into 24 equal-sized pieces and roll them into balls. Set aside.

2. Lightly flour your work surface and spread out the puff pastry sheets, smoothing them gently. In a small bowl, whisk the milk and egg together to make an egg wash. Brush tops of the pastry sheets with the egg wash, setting any leftovers aside to use later. Cut each pastry sheet into 12 squares.

3. Place one meatball into the center of each pastry square. Fold the corners of the pastry square over the meatball and pinch the edges together to make a parcel. Repeat with the rest of the squares.

4. Preheat the oven to 375°F and lightly grease a baking pan. Place the pastries on the pan, leaving about an inch between them, and brush each with the remaining egg wash.

5. Bake until golden brown and cooked through, about 20 minutes.

6. Meanwhile, make the dip: In a mixing bowl, combine the cucumbers, yogurt and garlic, and mix well. Taste and mix in the salt. Put the dip in a serving bowl.

7. Serve the puffballs warm, with the yogurt dip on the side.

AUBERGINE: EGGPLANT

The earliest mention of eggplant is in a Chinese text from about 1,500 years ago. The first description we have of how to grow the plant is in an Arabic text from the twelfth century. Eggplant is believed to have been grown in the Middle East at least four or five centuries earlier, as it was brought by the Arabs to Spain in the eighth century. The name aubergine is from the Arabic, *al-bidinjan*. This word in turn comes from Persian by way of Sanskrit, a language once spoken in India.

WHAT'S IN A NAME?

Baba is a fond name often used for an older person, like dad or grandpa. *Ghanoush* is believed by some to be a person's name, but I think there is a much better explanation. Most Arabic words have a three-letter root, which you can look up in a dictionary. In this case it would be *ghanaj*. This root word does not appear in today's dictionaries. By taking a look in the dictionaries from several hundred years ago, you can find the word *ghanaj*. There it means to tease or tempt. In other words, *baba ghanoush* could mean a tempting dish for an elderly person.

Student of the Marshland

It wasn't so long ago, though maybe longer than we know, a boy called Hassan spent his days fishing for carp in the marshland beyond the city. In autumn, the marsh would fill with geese arriving from the Far North. In the spring flocks of flamingos, pelicans and herons would settle along the waterway to nest and feed. Occasionally, Hassan would see an African darter, black against the blue water. Among the reeds were gray warblers and marbled ducks. In early summer, families of otters slid from the banks into streams to hunt for carp.

Most mornings, when Hassan left home for the marshland, he would hurry past a group of children who were sitting and listening to an elderly man with a beard and turban. He wondered how they kept themselves so still and quiet when there was so much to see and do.

One day, the children stopped Hassan.

"Why don't you join us in class?" they asked.

"I have fish to catch and birds to watch in the marshland," he replied.

"Oh, so the wetlands are better than our classroom?" The children laughed.

Hassan smiled shyly, not sure what to say.

"You must come to our class," said a bright young boy. "You'll learn from our master all about life and nature and the wonders of the natural world."

"And where did your master learn all of this?"

"From the many books he has read," the boy replied.

"And once you have learned it all, what can you do with it?" asked Hassan.

"We can teach it and maybe even write books about it for others to learn."

"But the marshland is life and nature," said Hassan. "And I prefer to live it for myself, rather than learn it from somebody else's words in a book." He swung his fishing rod over his shoulder and hurried for the trail to the wetlands.

··

As experience is gained not taught; experience without teaching is better than teaching without experience.

Sayyadeyat Samak (Broiled Fish)

Many coastal cities of the Arab world have their own special way of preparing fish. Some fishmongers will even have an oven in a side room. After buying your fish, you can, for an extra charge, ask for it to be cooked according to one of their specialty recipes. The recipe below calls for harissa, a Moroccan-style hot sauce (see page 56), which comes in mild or regular. If you don't like spicy foods, leave it out.

SERVES 4

INGREDIENTS

2 large potatoes, peeled and thinly sliced

4 white fish fillets like cod, haddock, tilapia, grouper or snapper

2 tomatoes, thinly sliced

1 onion, thinly sliced

1 lemon, thinly sliced

1 teaspoon salt

1 teaspoon ground black pepper

1 teaspoon cumin

1 teaspoon ground coriander

4 garlic cloves, minced

handful of chopped parsley, to garnish

Sauce

¼ cup extra-virgin olive oil

½ cup white vinegar

¼ cup freshly squeezed lemon juice

2 tablespoons tomato paste

1 tablespoon mild green harissa sauce (optional)

PREPARATION

1. Preheat the oven to 375°F.

2. First, make the sauce: in a mixing bowl, combine the olive oil, vinegar, lemon juice, tomato paste and harissa sauce (if using) and mix well.

3. Arrange the potatoes in the bottom of a roasting pan in a single layer. Spread about one-third of the sauce over the top and bake for 20 to 25 minutes until the potatoes have softened and are almost cooked through.

4. Remove the pan from the oven and turn the oven temperature down to 200°F. Place the fish fillets on top of the potatoes, then top them with the remaining sauce. Arrange the tomato, onion and lemon slices on top, and cover with foil. Return to the oven until the fish and vegetables are cooked through, 15 to 20 minutes.

5. Remove the foil and switch your oven to broil for 5 minutes to brown the top, if you like. Garnish with chopped parsley and serve.

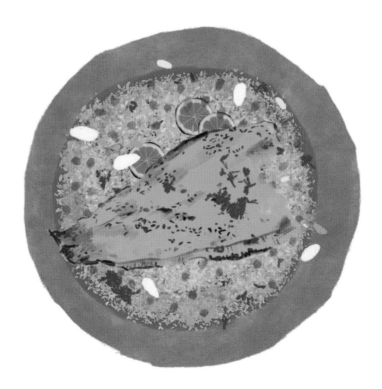

Tamar Hindi (Tamarind Cooler)

Sweet and tangy, the dried fruit of the tamarind tree is made into a drink sold by street vendors in much of the Middle East and North Africa. It is a popular summer thirst quencher. Tamarind is also used in recipes for chicken and fish, as well as for flavoring ice cream and desserts. You can find tamarind paste in blocks in the international or spice aisles of most supermarkets, as well as online.

SERVES 2

INGREDIENTS

1 cup tamarind paste

6 cups water

2 tablespoons sugar, or to taste

1 tablespoon rose water

PREPARATION

1. Break up the tamarind into 1-inch pieces and put them in a saucepan with 3 cups of the water. Bring to a boil over medium heat, then simmer for 5 minutes to soften the pulp. Turn off the heat and add the remaining 3 cups of water. Cover and leave to steep for a couple of hours until the liquid is dark and flavorful.

2. Strain through a fine-mesh strainer into a jug and discard the pulp.

3. Add the sugar and rose water to the jug, mix well, then chill in the refrigerator and serve cold.

TAMARIND

Tamar hind are the Arabic words from which the English
name tamarind is taken. The words mean "Indian dates." The
tamarind tree is believed to have originally come from Africa.
Its fruit develops inside long brittle pods. The pulp from the
broken pods can be eaten fresh or dried and stored for later
use. The flavor is sweet, but tart. Tamarind can be used as a
base for making jams, chutneys and marinades, as well as
added to sauces and stews. The pulp has a strong flavor, so a
little can go a long way.

The Brickmaker's Hoard

"One day, and a fine day it had been," said Masoud, the brickmaker, to his daughter Maysa, "I was on my way home, having delivered a cartload of bricks to a builder in a city with many glass and carpet merchants. Often, on my way there and on my way back I would share a meal with other travelers. It was getting late, so I decided to stop in a grove of birch trees and tall grass."

Masoud told Maysa how he had unharnessed his mule and given it water and a bundle of fresh clover he had brought with him. With some broken branches and the straw left on his cart from packing the bricks, he lit a small fire to warm a dish of lentils, noodles and rice. It was then he was approached by a man who, he thought, had all the signs of being a scoundrel. Masoud decided to be friendly and he offered to share his meal with the stranger.

"What were you doing in the city?" asked the stranger as he tucked in.

"Delivering bricks."

"Yes," the stranger said. He could tell from the dust and straw on the cart. "You must have made a pretty profit."

Work was hard and profit margins were always tight for brickmakers, Masoud replied. This was why he sometimes had to travel far to deliver his bricks.

"Yes, yes," said the stranger, "you must have done very well and made a small fortune." He glanced about him as though to see where Masoud could have stashed his cash.

Once the meal was over, Masoud waited for the stranger to leave. But the man kept trying to strike up a conversation about Masoud's wealth, and how and where he lived. When it became clear to him the man would not leave, Masoud said it was getting late and he would need to get some sleep. Still, the man sat by the lantern Masoud had lit. He kept asking about the price of bricks in the city, how that compared with selling bricks in the village, and how many bricks Masoud had delivered.

Masoud broke off birch bark in thin strips to lay under ground-sheets, along with the straw, for himself and the stranger to sleep on. He put out the light and covered himself with a blanket by the side of the cart. He watched as the stranger did the same close by.

Several times during that night, Masoud told Maysa, he woke to the scuttling sound of the stranger moving around the mule and cart, peering and poking in the dark at the bundle of animal feed for the mule, and searching under and around the cart. The man's movements became more frantic as the night wore on.

"I knew he must have seen me in the city taking money from the builder, and had spent the best part of the day following me for a chance to rob me."

"Oh dear," Maysa said, "that must have been scary for you, baba."

With first light, Masoud rose and gathered his belongings onto the cart. The stranger woke at the sounds made by the mule.

He appeared tired and disheveled, exhausted by lack of sleep. Masoud waved goodbye to the ragged-looking stranger.

"Where did you hide the money?" Maysa asked.

"When I spread the groundsheets, I hid my purse among the birch barks and straw I laid for him to sleep on. He slept on it for the hour or so he was asleep. In the morning, I took it with the groundsheets when I left."

..

As opportunity may make a villain, so cunning in adversity can be a virtue.

Kushary (Lentil and Noodle Hodgepodge)

Restaurants in Cairo vie with one another to present the tastiest and most decorative dishes of *kushary* with a variety of garnishes and side dishes. It is so popular in Egypt, you will find many restaurants serving only this one dish. The great thing about kushary is you can vary the quantities of ingredients to add more of what you like and less of what you don't. So, don't be afraid to experiment. Kushary is a great way to use up leftover cooked rice, lentils and pasta.

SERVES 4

INGREDIENTS

1 cup elbow pasta

1 cup cooked or canned chickpeas (drained and rinsed)

Sauce

2 tablespoons olive or vegetable oil

2–4 garlic cloves, minced

1 teaspoon ground coriander

1 teaspoon cumin

1 teaspoon ground black pepper

1 teaspoon smoked paprika

14 oz can tomato sauce

2 tablespoons vinegar, or to taste

Lentils

2 tablespoons olive or vegetable oil

1 teaspoon ground cumin

1 teaspoon ground coriander

2 garlic cloves, minced

1 cup brown lentils

Rice

1 cup short-grain rice, rinsed and drained

1 teaspoon ground cumin

1 teaspoon ground coriander

Fried Onions

4 tablespoons olive or vegetable oil

1 large onion, coarsely chopped

Garnish

chopped cilantro or parsley (optional)

salt and ground black pepper

PREPARATION

1. First, make the sauce: In a sauté pan, heat 2 tablespoons of the oil over medium heat. Add the garlic, cumin, coriander, paprika and black pepper, and cook, stirring, until fragrant. Add the tomato sauce and simmer, uncovered, for 10 minutes until thickened. Stir in the vinegar, taste, and add more vinegar or some salt if needed. Set aside in the pan.

2. Next, cook the lentils: In a separate saucepan, heat the oil and add the cumin, coriander, garlic, 1½ teaspoons of salt and ½ teaspoon of pepper. Cook, stirring, for a minute or so until fragrant, then add 1 cup of water and bring to a boil. Add the lentils and cook over medium heat until soft, about 30 minutes. Drain any remaining liquid and keep the lentils warm in the pot.

3. Meanwhile, cook the rice: Put the rice in a saucepan and add the cumin, coriander, ½ teaspoon of salt and ½ teaspoon of black pepper. Pour in 1½ cups of water and bring to a boil, then turn down the heat to low and simmer, covered, for 20 minutes or until the rice is tender and the water has been absorbed. Set aside in the pot.

4. Next, boil the elbow pasta in salted water until cooked, but still a little firm (al dente). This usually takes about 12 minutes, but check the instructions on the package. Drain the pasta and place it in a large serving bowl.

5. To prepare the fried onions, place olive or vegetable oil in a frying pan. Heat until the oil shimmers and fry the onions until they are golden and crispy, about 10 minutes (you may need to do this in batches). Remove the onions from the pan and set aside.

6. Add the lentils, rice and chickpeas to the pasta in the serving bowl and mix well. Reheat the sauce, if necessary, and pour it on top. Decorate with the fried onions and some chopped parsley or cilantro if you like.

WHERE DID KUSHARY COME FROM?

Kushary is Egypt's national dish. It has a little of everything from everywhere smothered in a spicy Egyptian tomato sauce. Its origins are recent, but how it came about is a bit of a mystery. It likely developed in the middle of the nineteenth century. At that time, a large number of foreign workers arrived from Europe, as well as from India and Africa to work in Egypt. The dish is a tasty combination, or fusion, of several different cultures.

THE FLAVORFUL SEED

Cumin is a small seed with an ancient pedigree. Its name comes from Arabic by way of Akkadian, the language of ancient Babylon. Cumin seeds have been found at archeological digs in Syria and Egypt and dated to the second millennium BCE. In ancient Egypt, cumin was used as an ingredient in mummification. Nowadays, in countries such as Egypt and Morocco, cumin is often added to the table in its own grinder, as are salt and pepper. Cumin can be made into a tea-like infusion in hot water. For extra flavor and aroma, the seeds can be added whole to rice as it is being cooked.

The Sultan and His Wazir

There was once, as once we were told, a mighty king who ruled over a great city called Kairouan, in Tunisia. This sultan had a large and jolly *wazir*, or chief advisor. Whenever the sultan asked him about anything, the wazir would say, "All is well, Your Majesty. All is well."

The sultan had a large garden in his palace. Among the many fruit trees was a tall pomegranate. One summer, with the tree's fruit ripening, the sultan said he wanted to taste a fresh pomegranate. The wazir bent low, and the sultan climbed on his back. As the sultan reached for a branch, he lost his balance and fell.

The wazir hurried to help the sultan, saying, "Oh dear, Your Majesty. All is well. All is well."

"No, all is not well!" shouted the sultan in a rage.

"Yes, but indeed all is well, Your Majesty," repeated the distressed wazir. "All is well."

The sultan ordered the wazir locked up. "I'll keep him in the dungeons until he stops saying that silly nonsense of all is well."

A few days later, the sultan went on his annual tour of the kingdom. This time he decided to cross from the coastal plains to renew his claim to the desert lands. One morning, he woke early and decided to ride his horse and enjoy the sunrise and the fresh desert air. He stopped when he realized he was far from his camp and should turn back. Just then, he found himself lifted from the saddle and suspended high above the ground. Glancing up, he saw he was being held by his cloak, which was pinched between the fingers of a very scary-looking giant ghoul.

"A nice morsel," said the ghoul. "I'll save you for my sweetheart." In several great steps, the ghoul carried the sultan to a cave in the side of a mountain. The ghoul called out, "Sweetie pie!" and a second large and even scarier-looking ghoul appeared.

"Here, darling," said the first ghoul. "I got you a delicious tidbit."

The second ghoul sniffed at the sultan with her big red nose, then shook her head. "No, dear, there's not enough meat on him to make a meatball."

"Oh, you're too persnickety." The ghoul tossed the sultan over his shoulder.

His Majesty went tumbling through the air and landed head first in a sand dune, close to where the ghoul had found him.

Once back in his palace, the sultan thought maybe he'd been a little too hard on the wazir. He asked his cook to prepare the wazir's favorite dish of honey-glazed meatballs and ordered his release. As the wazir ate, the sultan told him of his encounter with the ghouls. "But now tell me, how does it feel to have been imprisoned for so long in the dungeons?"

"Oh all is well, Your Majesty. All is well," replied the wazir in a cheery tone.

"How can you say that?"

"All is well, Your Majesty. Had I not been in your dungeon, the ghoul would have kidnapped us both and very likely made a meatball of me.

Then, Your Majesty, all would not have been well. Not well at all."
He shook his head and popped a meatball into his mouth.

..

*Some things may bring good luck, but bad luck
can sometimes be good for something.*

Kufta Assaleyah (Honey-Glazed Meatballs)

Kufta is the Arabic word for meatballs. Kufta can be cooked in tomato sauce, or skewered and then grilled or broiled and served as kebab, often with side dishes of hummus (page 36) and baba ghanoush (page 78). In this recipe, kufta is cooked in a delicious, sticky honey-pomegranate sauce and can be served with rice or couscous. You can find pomegranate molasses in most grocery stores.

SERVES 4

INGREDIENTS

1 lb ground beef

1 onion, finely chopped

1 large garlic clove, minced

1 cup finely chopped parsley

1 teaspoon ground cumin

1 teaspoon ground coriander

1 teaspoon ground cinnamon

1 teaspoon salt

2 tablespoons olive or vegetable oil

Glaze

2 tablespoons honey

¼ cup pomegranate molasses

107

PREPARATION

1. In a large mixing bowl, combine the ground beef, onion, garlic, parsley, cumin, coriander, cinnamon and salt. Shape the mixture into 16 evenly sized meatballs.

2. In a large frying pan, heat the oil over medium heat. Cook the meatballs, turning them from time to time, until browned all over and cooked through, 10 to 15 minutes.

3. In a small bowl, mix the honey and pomegranate molasses to make a glaze. Pour the glaze evenly over the meatballs, stirring them until they are well coated. Turn down the heat to low and cook until the glaze has thickened and is sticky, about 5 minutes.

4. Serve with rice or couscous.

WILD HONEY

The earliest images of people gathering honey are cave drawings from 10,000 years ago in India and East Africa. Wall carvings in Egyptian tombs from 4,500 years ago are the first evidence of people farming bees for honey. The ancient Egyptians used clay pots for beehives. Egypt became a major producer of honey for food and medicine. Egypt continues to produce more honey than any other country in the Middle East and North Africa. However, the most prized and expensive honey is from Yemen. A honey store in Yemen's capital, Sanaa, may stock hundreds of different varieties of honey.

The Kindly Old Man

In a time when all men had moustaches and all cats had whiskers, Jawad was a traveling merchant who bought and sold dates. He had little time for the worries of others, thinking what little good they would do him when he was always so busy. From the wide variety of dates grown, he preferred to trade in the dry and firm *Thoory*, the red and crunchy *Zahidi* and the sweet, dark *Halawy*. For the right price he would also buy and sell the chewy *Barhi* or *Deglet Noor*.

One year, early in the season, Jawad returned to Mosul. He had just negotiated the terms for the year's shipment with a broker in Damascus. As heavy rains had flooded his usual route, he decided to take an unfamiliar road home. He became lost, and in the failing light, his horse stumbled on rough ground. Jawad fell, spraining his ankle and grazing his arms and knees.

On the road ahead, he saw an old man. He called to him, asking if he knew of somewhere he could spend the night. The old man pointed to a light from a house a short distance away. At the door to the house, Jawad was met by a young woman who welcomed him in. She arranged for him to be fed and his horse stabled. Jawad's cuts and bruises were treated and dressed, and he was offered a meal with stuffed date cookies for dessert. He was given a room to sleep in and a fresh set of clothes for the next day's travel.

For the next few seasons, Jawad journeyed to and from Damascus along his usual route. He always intended to return and thank his hostess for her kindness, but found that he was too busy. Finally, one year, he decided he could wait no longer. The crop had been good and he decided to give his hostess sacks of the best dates as a gift. While asking his way on the road, he was told the owner of the house had passed away. Deeply saddened, Jawad hurried to reach the house to offer his condolences. On arriving, he was surprised to see the young woman alive and well.

"Do you remember the elderly man who first showed you the way here?" asked the young woman. "He was the master of this house."

Jawad confessed he had barely noticed the old man. He felt regret at having missed his chance to thank him. It was only then he understood that intentions are no substitute for actions.

..

Postponing a good deed can make of the deed no deed at all.

Mamoul (Date-Filled Cookies)

Traditionally, *mamoul* or more correctly *m'amoul* (with the *'a* being an "a" sound from the back of the throat) is the dessert most popular at the end of Christian Lent and the Muslim feast of Eid after the month of Ramadan. Then, platters of the cookie are often exchanged among friends and neighbors. They are also served at weddings. The pastry-like dough is stuffed with dates and ground pistachios or walnuts and dusted with powdered sugar to make a special treat.

MAKES ABOUT 36

INGREDIENTS

Filling

1 lb pitted dates, chopped

½ cup water

½ teaspoon ground cinnamon

½ teaspoon ground nutmeg

¼ cup chopped pistachios (optional)

Dough

2 cups all-purpose flour

1 cup semolina

½ teaspoon *mahlab* or ground cardamom (optional)

¼ teaspoon salt

1 cup (8 oz) cold unsalted butter, cut into 1-inch cubes

2 tablespoons rose water

½ cup milk, or as needed

confectioner's sugar, for dusting

معمول

PREPARATION

1. First, make the filling: In a saucepan (preferably nonstick), combine the dates and water and stir over low heat until you have a sticky paste, 3 to 5 minutes. Let it cool, then mix in the cinnamon, nutmeg and pistachios, if using. Set aside.

2. For the dough: In a mixing bowl, combine the all-purpose flour, semolina, mahlab or cardamom and salt. Add the butter and rub it in with your fingers until you have an even grainy mixture.

3. Stir in the rose water, then gradually mix in the milk, a little at a time, kneading until it comes together and you have a soft dough.

4. Preheat the oven to 325°F. Grease two baking sheets with butter or line with parchment paper.

5. Pinch off about a tablespoon-size piece of dough and roll it into a ball. Using your thumb, press down on the dough ball to form a little bowl. Put a heaped teaspoon of date filling into the bowl and seal it by gently pushing the dough over the filling. Make sure all the filling is covered as evenly as you can manage. Repeat until you have used up all the dough and the filling, placing the cookies about an inch apart on a greased baking tray. Using a fork, carefully press shallow ridges or a crisscross design into the top of each cookie.

6. Bake until lightly golden on the bottom, 20 to 25 minutes. Be very careful not to let the cookies brown too much or they will dry out and their flavor will be spoiled. The mamoul will be soft when you remove them from the oven, but they will firm up as they cool. Once cooled, dust with the confectioner's sugar. Store leftovers in an airtight container.

Date Shake

SERVES 2

INGREDIENTS

¼ cup walnut pieces

½ cup chopped dates

½ cup lukewarm water

¼ teaspoon ground cinnamon

pinch kosher salt

1 cup vanilla ice cream

1 cup crushed ice

PREPARATION

1. If you like, toast the walnuts in a dry frying pan over medium heat, or on a baking pan in an oven preheated to 350°F, until golden brown, about 10 minutes. Set aside to cool.

2. Place the chopped dates in a small bowl and add the water. Set aside to soak for 10 to 20 minutes.

3. Pour the dates along with their soaking water into a blender and add the walnuts, cinnamon and salt. Blend to a paste. Add the ice cream and crushed ice and blend until smooth. Pour the shake into 2 tall glasses.

عصير التمر

DATE VARIETIES

In North America and Europe, they say an apple a day keeps
the doctor away. In the Middle East, the advice is to eat seven
dates a day. Dates are rich in iron, as well as in selenium, copper
and magnesium. They are also high in vitamins A, B and C.
The country that grows the most and probably best dates is
Iraq. They claim to have over a hundred different types. Some
countries have their own specialty dates. For example, the long
red Zahloul is only grown in Egypt, while the Sukkary is a
Saudi Arabian favorite.

Dates ripen on palm trees late in the summer. They come in
a variety of sweetness and softness. Some types are favorites
for eating raw:

Medjool: large fruit, sweet, moist and soft

Barhi: small fruit with a rich soft flavor

Halawi: soft honey flavor, with a name meaning "sweet"

Khadrawi: small, moist and orange in color

Dayri: large fruit with red skin that ripens to black

Other types are often used for cooking:

Deglet Noor: delicately flavored and dry, with an amber
or deep-brown skin

Thoory: sweet and dry with golden-brown flesh

Zahidi: medium-sized juicy fruit with a yellow skin

117

HERBS AND HERBALISTS

In the Middle East, many people still rely on alternative medicine along with modern medical practices. Over 250 different herbs are sold in today's marketplaces. Many are for cooking as well as for treating different ailments. The first drug stores were opened in Baghdad in the eighth century. They sold different herbs for making medicines. According to some sources, as many as 814 different plants were used to create the medicines sold in those stores.

MAHLAB: THE BITTER FRUIT

The mahlab cherry, also called the St. Lucie cherry, is native to the Middle East. Unlike most cherries, it is not grown for its fruit as much as it is for its seed. Once harvested, the stone of the cherry is collected and cracked to remove the soft kernel, which is then ground to a fine powder. The kernel tastes a bit like marzipan, a sweet made from almond paste. Mahlab has been used in cooking for thousands of years. It is mentioned in the ancient epic story of Gilgamesh, who traveled the world on a quest for the secret of how to live forever. In Arab recipes, it is usually used to give extra flavor when baking cookies, cakes and bread.

The Genie in the Sack

There was once, in a time gone by, a young woman named Heba who owned some land she sowed with durum wheat. She sold the wheat at markets in Oran, in what today is the country of Algeria, for people to buy and make into semolina, couscous, pastries and bread. One day, having gathered the wheat and milled the grain, she noticed a sack was missing from her storeroom. She called the workmen and asked if any of them had taken the sack of wheat. They all denied doing so.

That evening, sitting alone and sipping a drink of lime and mint, Heba had an idea. She called her workers to a meeting and showed them a sealed sack. "I got this sack from a holy man, with great magical powers, a *marabout*. Inside the sack is a genie. This jinn knows who stole the grain from the storeroom." She said she would place the sack in a dark room. The men were to enter one at a time and place an arm into the sack, then go wait against the far wall. The jinn would recognize who stole the sack of durum wheat and let her know.

One by one the men entered the room, then waited for the truth to be revealed. When all had gone through, Heba lit a lantern. She followed the last man into the room. She told the men to hold out their arms, then pointed to one of them and said, "You are the thief."

"Oh no, I am innocent," said the man. He pointed to his arm to show the jinn had not marked it.

"Look at the arms of your companions." Heba held the lantern close for him to see their arms were black, while his was not. "There was soot in the sack. Only the guilty person would not have put their arm in to test the jinn."

The man pleaded forgiveness.

Heba made him return the sack of wheat he had stolen and promise never to lie or steal again. But even so, it would be a long time before she could ever trust him.

..

If first a liar, then a thief. A liar and a thief will always come to grief.

Couscous Bilzbeeb (Couscous Pudding with Fruit & Raisins)

Couscous is a staple of many North African dishes. Famously, the competition for who makes the best couscous is between Moroccans and Tunisians. The rivalry can sometimes be intense.

SERVES 4

INGREDIENTS

¾ cup water

¼ teaspoon salt

¾ cup couscous

1½ cups milk

1 teaspoon vanilla

2 green cardamom pods

½ teaspoon ground cinnamon

4 tablespoons dried fruits like cherries, prunes and raisins, plus extra to decorate

1 tablespoon ground nuts, like almonds and pistachios, for garnish

Flavored syrup like maple syrup, to serve

PREPARATION

1. In a saucepan, bring the water to a boil. Stir in the salt, then the couscous, and remove from the heat. Cover and set aside for 10 minutes until the water has been absorbed. Stir using a fork to fluff up the grains.

2. Meanwhile, in another saucepan, combine the milk, vanilla, cardamom and cinnamon. Bring to a simmer and cook, stirring, over low heat for 10 minutes, until thickened. Be careful not to let it burn. Remove from heat and remove the cardamom pods. Mix in the dried fruit.

3. Place the couscous in a serving bowl and pour in the milk mixture. Set aside to cool until warm.

4. Transfer to serving bowls and decorate with nuts and raisins. Serve with syrup on the side.

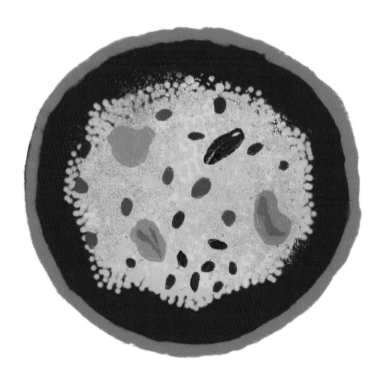

Lime and Mint Refresher

This refreshing drink is common across North Africa, from Egypt to Morocco. It is usually made with limes, but can also be made with lemons for a milder taste. When poured, it often forms a frothy crown that floats over the top of the ice.

SERVES 2

INGREDIENTS

4 limes or 2 large lemons

juice of 2 limes or 1 large lemon

4 cups cold water

handful fresh mint leaves

½–1 cup sugar, to taste

crushed ice, to serve

PREPARATION

1. Wash the limes or lemons well in warm water, then quarter them and remove any seeds.

2. Add the quarters (with their peel), to a blender and blend to a purée. Add the juice, water and mint leaves and blend well.

3. Strain the liquid into a pitcher. Taste and mix in sugar to your liking.

4. Serve over crushed ice in tall glasses, or refrigerate to serve later.

عصير الليمون

WHAT IS COUSCOUS?

The Arabic word *couscous* comes from the word *seksu* in
Amazigh, a people and a language spoken in North Africa.
The earliest traces of couscous were found inside ancient
graves from the Amazigh Kingdom of Numidia, in what is
today Algeria. Some of the earliest recipes for couscous are
found in a thirteenth-century Arabic cookbook called *The
Book of Reaching the Beloved*—a title that suggests the best
way to capture a person's heart is through their stomach.

The Dream Garden

There was once, in an age long gone, in a city on the coast of the Arabian Sea, a grouchy king who had two sullen sons and a loving daughter, Soraya. One night, the king dreamed of a beautiful garden with trees of lapis lazuli and fruit of glittering green emeralds, white sapphires and red rubies.

The next morning, when the king woke, he could not stop thinking of the garden. He called his two sons and daughter and told them he wished for the jewels he'd seen in his dream. If they loved him, they would find the garden and bring him the gems.

The eldest son proudly dressed himself, as only a prince could, in a beautiful gown of silk. He saddled his horse with the finest leather and clipped to his heels silver stirrups. He set off with his group of courtiers. They were gone for several days before the courtiers returned to say they had taken leave of their prince, as they were sure no jeweled garden could ever be found. It was all a fantasy the grouchy king had dreamed.

"Dreams give wings to fools," they whispered to one another.

"Golden dreams make sleeping men wake up greedy," others murmured.

After several more days with no word from the prince, the second son, in a morose mood, dressed in gowns almost as fine as his brother's. He set off with his companions to find the jeweled garden.

Weeks later, the courtiers returned to say they had given up the search. Their prince had decided to continue his quest alone for his lost brother. As for the garden of gems, they were certain there could be no such place in any corner of the kingdom. They spoke of ghouls and monsters and silly riddles, and how much they hated being out of the palace and in the dirty, dusty world of common folk.

"Dreams of sweet desserts, like *kunafa* and *qatayef*, cannot satisfy anybody's hunger," they muttered, nodding agreement with one another.

When, after a few more weeks, her brothers had not returned, Soraya decided she should go in search of them. She rose early and dressed to disguise herself as a simple stable boy, folding her long hair under a plain turban. She saddled her horse and set off alone. She stopped in villages and hamlets to ask if anybody had seen her brothers or knew of the garden of gems.

After weeks of searching, Soraya stopped at a house made of chicken bones and feathers. An old woman was feeding chicks in the yard. Soraya said she was lost and needed directions.

"First deserve, then desire," the woman said, scattering grain for the chicks. "You answer me a riddle and I'll tell you the way." Soraya agreed, and the old woman asked, "What is a town with walls of straw and homes without windows and doors?"

Soraya thought for a moment then answered, "A nest is made of straw, and eggs are homes without windows or doors."

The old woman laughed and asked, "What is your question?"

Soraya said she was looking for her brothers who had gone in search of the garden of gems.

"For that you must ask the ghoul who lives in the wild lands. She is both vain and bad tempered," the old woman said. "You must praise her before she sees you, otherwise she'll have your bones for toothpicks."

Soraya set off again and rode on and on into the wild lands until she saw a large and fearsome-looking ghoul, monstrous in size, leaning against a hillock.

"Peace be upon you, sister ghoul. You are so beautiful in the sunlight," Soraya called out.

"Had your greeting not come before your appearing," growled the ghoul, "I'd have crunched you and munched you."

"The blue of the sky matches your lovely eyes. The green of the hills contrasts so well with your fine complexion," Soraya said.

The ghoul blushed.

Soraya told the ghoul of the quest to find her two brothers.

"It's a dangerous place you're going," the ghoul said. She told Soraya the garden belonged to the jinn. It was hidden inside a mountain.

"How do I get there?"

"A gardener arrives there every night. Watch and listen and you will find out."

Soraya set off. She rode for days until she reached the mountain described by the ghoul. When she arrived, she hid among the rocks, waiting for the gardener to appear. As the sun was setting, she saw a man approaching the mountain.

"Rubies and lapis," the man shouted. "Emeralds, ivory and ebony. Open your stone door." With a loud creaking sound, the mountain cracked open, letting out a rainbow of colors. The man walked inside the mountain and it closed behind him. Soraya waited and waited. It was almost dawn before the man came out and went along his way.

When all was quiet and not a thing stirring, Soraya went to the mountainside and repeated the words she'd heard. "Rubies and lapis. Emeralds, ivory and ebony. Open your stone door." The mountain creaked open and Soraya went in. She saw she was in a garden of blue lapis trees. On the branches hung large sapphires, emeralds and rubies. Fluttering above her were macaws, toucans, cockatoos, parrots and parakeets and all kinds of other birds, many she couldn't name. They were as colorful as the jewels on the trees. She filled her saddlebag with gems. She was about to go when she heard the birds

twittering, "Let us out, let us out. We want to go home. We want to go home." As she looked closer, she saw some of the birds had human faces. She recognized the face of her younger brother, a blue parakeet, and of her older brother, a red-and-black toucan.

Soraya ordered the mountain to open by saying the magic words.

"Hurry, hurry," she called to the birds, "before the gardener returns."

As they flew out, the spell that had turned them into birds broke and they became human again.

It took Soraya and her brothers many days to return to the king's palace. When they arrived there, they found the kingdom in disarray. The king was said to be very ill, consumed by remorse over the loss of his sons and daughter. At the palace gates, the guards refused to let them in. Soraya and her brothers were so ragged the guards did not believe they could be the princess and princes. Soraya opened her saddlebag and showed the guards the jewels, as large as oranges and apples. She told them these were a gift for the king. They quickly admitted her to the throne room, where she laid the gems at the foot of the king. "Your majesty, these are the precious stones you dreamed of from the magic garden."

The king gazed at the jewels with indifference. "For these shiny stones I've lost two sons and a daughter, each more precious to me than all the gems you could fetch."

The two princes came forward and wiped the thick layers of dust from their faces. Recognizing them, the king was joyful.

"But what of my daughter?" he asked. "What has happened to her?"

Soraya removed her turban and shook her head, releasing her hair to fall about her shoulders.

That evening the kingdom rejoiced at the return of the king's sons and daughter. The festivities went on for days. Soraya and her brothers took turns telling their stories to the king and courtiers, who listened in amazement at all they heard.

··

The riches of the heart cannot be stolen, only wasted. Their loss cannot be replaced.

Quick Kunafa

Kunafa is a popular dessert all over the Arab world, but the best kunafa is said to be made in the city of Nablus in Palestine, using *Akkawi* or *Nabulsi* cheese and flavored with local oranges and pistachios. *Nabulsi* and *Akkawi* are specialty cheeses not easily found at most stores. So for this recipe, we use a mixture of ricotta and mozzarella, which are easier to find and almost as good.

SERVES 8

INGREDIENTS

1 lb package shredded filo pastry (*kataifi*), defrosted

1½ cups (12 oz) melted ghee or butter, plus extra for greasing

2 teaspoons turmeric or saffron (for color, optional)

1½ cups whole milk ricotta cheese

1 cup shredded mozzarella cheese

ground pistachios, to decorate

Syrup

1 cup water

1 teaspoon freshly squeezed lemon juice

1 cup sugar or honey (orange blossom honey is often used)

1 tablespoon rose water

PREPARATION

1. First make the syrup: In a saucepan, combine the water, lemon juice and sugar or honey and bring to a boil, then turn down the heat and simmer, stirring, until the sugar or honey has dissolved, 5 minutes. Remove from the heat and stir in the rose water. Set aside to cool.

2. Put the shredded filo pastry in a food processor and pulse until you have 1- to 2-inch pieces. Place them in a bowl and pour in the melted butter and, if using, add turmeric or saffron. Mix well with your fingers until all of the pastry is coated.

3. Preheat the oven to 350°F and grease a 9- by 13-inch cake pan or baking dish with butter.

4. Spread half of the filo mixture on the base of the pan and pat it down with the back of a spoon to form a firm base.

5. In a mixing bowl, combine the ricotta and grated mozzarella cheeses, and dollop this mixture over the pastry in the pan. Using a spatula or moistened hands, gently spread the cheese over the pastry so you have an even layer.

6. Sprinkle the rest of the filo mixture over the cheese until it is completely covered, and pat down gently.

7. Bake for 15 to 20 minutes until the cheese has melted and the filo pastry is golden and crispy.

8. Pour as much of the cooled syrup as you like over the warm kunafa (any extra can be served on the side). Decorate the top of the kunafa with pistachios and serve warm.

Qatayef Asafeeri (Cream-Filled Pancakes)

Kunafa's rival for the most popular Arab dessert is probably qatayef, a filled pancake that is drizzled with sugar syrup. One popular version is stuffed with ground nuts and deep-fried before soaking in syrup. In this version, the pancakes are filled with thickened cream and served with syrup and pistachios without the deep-frying.

SERVES 4–6

INGREDIENTS

Filling
1 tablespoon milk

2 teaspoons cornstarch

2 cups heavy cream

1 teaspoon rose water

Batter
1 cup all-purpose flour

1 cup fine semolina

2 tablespoons sugar

pinch of salt

1 teaspoon baking powder

½ teaspoon instant yeast

2½ cups water

½ cup (4 oz) butter, for cooking

Topping
2 cups sugar syrup (page 136) or honey, or to taste

¼ cup ground pistachios

pinch saffron, to decorate (optional)

PREPARATION

1. First, make the filling: In a small saucepan, combine the milk and cornstarch and stir over low heat until you have a smooth paste. Add the cream and rose water and cook, stirring, until the mixture has thickened and starts to bubble, about 5 minutes. Be careful not to let it burn. Pour the mixture into a bowl and refrigerate until it sets, about 1 hour.

2. Meanwhile, make the pancake batter: In a mixing bowl, combine the flour, semolina, sugar, salt, baking powder and yeast. Gradually mix in the water until fully incorporated, then cover the bowl with a clean dish towel and set aside in a warm place for 30 minutes.

3. When you are ready to make your pancakes, melt about a tablespoon of butter in a frying pan over medium heat. Once hot, pour in 2 tablespoons of batter at a time to form pancakes about 3 inches in diameter. Be careful not to crowd the pan.

4. Let the pancakes cook until bubbles appear all over the top and the surface is dry. Do not flip the pancakes over, since this will make them brittle and difficult to fold.

5. Using a spatula, transfer the pancakes to a flat surface without stacking them (otherwise they will stick together). Cover them with a clean dish towel to keep them from drying out while you cook the rest of the pancakes. Add more butter to pan as needed. You should end up with 16 pancakes.

6. Scoop about a tablespoon of cream filling into the center of each pancake. Fold the pancakes over the filling into a semicircle, then press the edges together along one side, leaving one end open. Sprinkle some of the ground pistachios on the cream filling on the open end.

7. Drizzle syrup or honey over the qatayef and sprinkle more of the ground pistachios on top. You can add a few threads of saffron for color and flavor. Serve with extra syrup or honey on the side.

A NOTE ON KUNAFA AND QATAYEF

Kunafa is a name that comes from the Coptic, or Ancient Egyptian, word for cake. The earliest mention of kunafa can be found in the stories of *The Thousand and One Nights*. The cream-filled pancakes are called *qatayef asafeeri*, or bird pancakes. The earliest recipe for qatayef is in the tenth-century cookbook by al-Warraq (see page 10). According to some, the French word *crêpe*—the delicious wafer-thin pancake—likely comes from the Arabic word qatayef.

THE GOLDEN SPICE

Saffron or *zafaran* is an expensive spice. Ounce for ounce, it is more precious than gold. It is made from the red and yellow stigma and styles of a species of the crocus flower. It is thought to have been originally grown in ancient Iraq sometime in the Bronze Age. The ancient Sumerians of Mesopotamia used saffron for medical remedies and for magical potions. Saffron was also used to color fabric. There are references to saffron in Assyrian texts from the seventh century BCE. In ancient Egypt, Queen Cleopatra used saffron to scent her bathwater. Eighth-century Arab farmers were believed to have brought the saffron crocus to Spain, where it has been grown ever since.

In Happiness and Health

There are several words in Arabic for story. There is *rewaya*, which comes from a root word meaning to irrigate or to embellish. It most often means a long story such as a novel. There is also *qissah*, which is a word meaning to trace a path or follow a track. It can also mean to cut or be brief. This is the word often used for a short story.

The stories in this book would more accurately be called *hadduta*. The roots of this word are a little more mysterious than either rewaya or qissah. One explanation is that it comes from *hadd*, which means limits. In other words, it is a limited story, or a short-short story. But it could also mean a story that is just on the edge of being believable. Other meanings are also possible. One is that it comes from the word for the pupil of an eye. So, you could say, it is a story that holds your attention. Or maybe, to use a common English expression, a hadduta is a story that makes your eyes pop out. Another possible root meaning is the term for a nursery rhyme. Yet another is from the word for an event or a happening. If we roll all these possible meanings together, we could say a hadduta is a short tale that enchants and instructs all at the same time. Possibly, we could also call it a pleasurable parable or a bewitching fable.

Of these bewitchments, the story of the wise child is popular across the Arab world. The child may be a boy (often called Hassan) or a girl (sometimes called Malika) who outsmarts an adult. There are also trickster stories, whose hero may be called Goha, Mullah Nasruddin or Abu Nawas. These tales usually rely on a play of words or a joke taken too far. Goha and his son are a type of story that sits somewhere between the trickster and the wise-child story. Animal tales may involve a lesson to be learned. Often, so do stories of adults behaving badly or selfishly. Magical stories, similar to those in *The Thousand and One Nights*, often involve wizards and jinn with the occasional ghoul for good measure. In some stories, a distinction is drawn between jinn and ghoul. The ghouls are sometimes described as evil jinn, though more usually they are a separate species, and are often female. Jinn are flame-like creatures with magical powers and the ability to slip in and out of place and time. They can be any gender or form you can imagine.

As children, many of us heard our first hadduta from our mothers and aunts, who often heard the stories, as children, told to them by their own mothers and aunts. These are the stories whose flavors we have tried to give you a taste of in this cookbook—flavors we hope you will rediscover and enjoy by trying the recipes.

When people invite you to join them for a meal anywhere in the Arab world, they will say *"Bil hanna wal shiffa,"* which means "In happiness and health." And so, as we have arrived at the end of this Arab fairy tale feast, we wish you both *hanna* and *shiffa* and hope you enjoyed our offerings.

KARIM ALRAWI

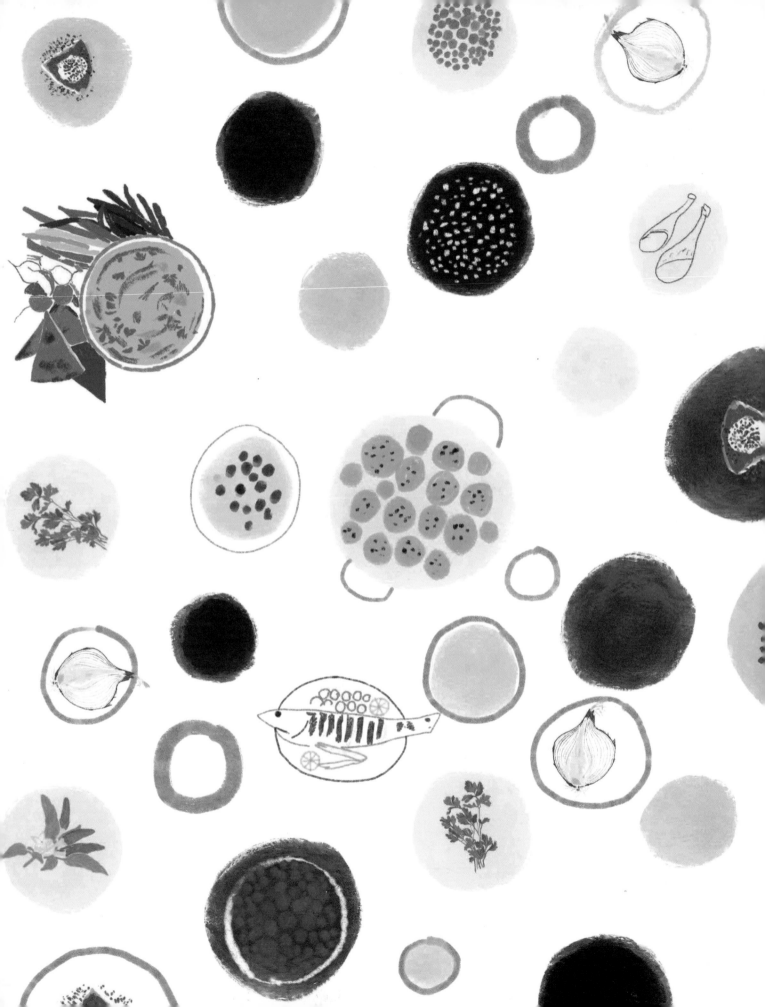